Big Dreams Small Suitcase

D1616049

By Maryam Ebrahimi
Illustrated by Farshid M. Amani
Edited by Panteha Healey and Famy Chavosh

I hope this book can be the train that takes you to the clouds.
The clouds could sit upon and go so high up into the sky,
where you can reach the city of your wishes.
The city that your hopes and dreams lay.

Maryam Ebrahimi. 2021

To all the immigrants who left their motherlands,
willingly or unwillingly.
The ones who left behind their memories,
their homes,
their families,
their friends,
their college degrees,
their careers,
their mother tongues,
their childhood dreams,
and, for some, even their self-confidence.
All left behind in their old cities or towns,
but never truly forgotten,
as they start from scratch somewhere new,
building a better life.

The loud cries of the just-born baby girl filled the delivery room. Darya smiled wide hearing her new baby, a smile much bigger and brighter than ever before. She felt as though this happiness somehow differed from all the other happiness in the world. Her entire being was held within two eyes, eyes that only wanted to gaze upon the face of her newborn baby girl. It was a face that Darya had been waiting to see for months.

Those months had felt like an eternity, with even a few seconds of it feeling like years. In the past few months, Darya had imagined looking at her baby's face so many times. But this was the first time she could actually stare at her, intently, fascinated by how familiar she looked. And what a dreamy experience it was.

The moment the baby girl got a glimpse of Darya's face, she stopped crying, fell silent and stared up at her mother with big, gleaming eyes.

Darya had a strange feeling, as though she was floating above the clouds, curiously looking down at her baby girl. The little baby continued to look up at her mother, but slowly her small eyes seemed to tire and she closed them, drifting off to sleep.

While watching her baby girl sleep in quiet bliss, Darya slowly floated back into the clouds of her own dreams.

The clouds enveloped her, carrying her up higher and higher. She floated so far up that she found herself arriving upon a place within her memories where she could relive her own childhood.

Darya looked around and saw that her memories were playing out in the form of a train, a train with a thousand train cars moving slowly and continuously. The train cars were passing in front of Darya's eyes, one after the other. Any time she could, Darya would peek through the train car windows and catch a glimpse of her own childhood face covered in a big smile, a smile which was so ever-present that it was now a signature on her face. Inside one of the train cars, Darya saw a tiny ladybug, which was making its way across her childhood shoes.

This recalled the simple joys of her childhood, when seeing a ladybug or butterfly could be the highlight of her day. It was amazingly easy for little Darya to feel happiness from even the most trivial happenings around her. She was thrilled whenever the flowers blossomed, when the buds bloomed, when the clouds took on different strange shapes in the sky, when she could hear the rhythm of the rain hitting her window, or when she found a delicate bird nest with tiny, freshly laid eggs. Even though they had been so simple, each of these instances had been so precious to her and had filled her life with so much joy and laughter.

While caught up in these thoughts, the next train car rolled slowly by. Darya shook her head and laughed. This train car brought with it a particularly enjoyable childhood memory that she absolutely loved. Inside the train car, little Darya was completely surrounded by colorful gifts.

Darya remembered a time in her childhood when she liked to imagine a giant basket filled to the brim with gifts, each a colorful box that she had patiently wrapped with beautiful colored paper.

In these gift boxes were things that were extremely valuable, but none of them could be bought with money.

They held pieces of her happiness that she wanted to share with her friends, like a wish, some raindrops, or a ray of sunlight.

Darya's favorite gift was a big fluffy cloud that you could sit upon which would take you so high up into the sky that you could see the entire world from there.

Darya still had not tired of the sweet memory of those gifts when a loud noise demanded her attention.

From the next train car she could hear the shouts of children and finally came to see it was full of her childhood friends.

The sound of boisterous, happy shouting filled the air.

She remembered days when you laughed for no reason, when you could run freely and without direction, when grown-ups didn't ask you what you were running towards or if you had reached it. Darya remembered how much she loved to play happily when she was a child, to dance and sing and talk loudly.

She longed to spend more time in this train car, but once again the train kept rolling and she knew she wouldn't have enough time to get to each of her memories one by one.

The next train car was completely silent. In it she saw herself as a little girl, sitting calmly and quietly in a corner with her eyes closed.

Darya was filled with a warm memory -- as much as she had loved to shout and play and run as a child, she would also often sit quietly and reflect on her biggest hopes and dreams.

These hopes and dreams were so special to her that they took the shape of an imaginary friend that lived in her heart.

This friend would light the way for Darya, helping her to see a path through the darkness all the way up to the clouds, where her hopes and dreams lay.

Little Darya had heard in storybooks that there was a place in the sky where people could live with their wishes, and to get there, she would have to find these magical clouds and ride them up to find her own hopes and dreams.

The only way to reach this place was on these clouds, and Darya knew that if she found them, she could reach any dream.

Thinking of this desire reminded Darya of her mom and just how much she missed her. Darya was happy that she could walk within the memories of this train because she knew she would find her mom within one of the train cars.

She rose quickly and searched each of the remaining train cars one by one.

Eventually, she found her mom who was, as usual, heads down busy sewing clothes. Darya longed so badly to hold the train up and get her fill of staring at her mother.

As she stood there, Darya remembered that her mom was the best seamstress in the neighborhood.

She could weave the most beautiful things, and friends, neighbors, and relatives would visit from near and far to learn how to sew and knit from her.

Darya's mother was also the best cook in the family -- but more important than any of these skills was her ability to tell the best stories.

It was while Darya was lost in these thoughts that the sound of the train distracted her once again, pulling her away from memories of being with her mother. The next train car was full of guests, laughing and talking. While many were friends from Darya's childhood, there were family members and neighbors as well, all sitting around her mother and listening to her magical stories. Her stories transported you to distant lands and allowed you to meet many new friends. Sometimes you'd even meet people who had astonishing, almost magical powers.

Darya remembered that in one of these stories, her favorite characters would take all the happiness in the world and divide it amongst everyone equally.

The happiness would be wrapped up in beautiful packages and everyone could pick whichever package was their favorite color, knowing that regardless of which package they received, the happiness contained within it would be neither less nor more than what the next person received.

Even though it was nice to stay in this world of story-telling, this train car inevitably passed as well.

Darya closed her eyes and thought about how great it would be to remain with her imaginary friends from those beautiful stories.

While her eyes were closed, several train cars full of memories passed by.

There wasn't time for Darya to look closely into each of them, but suddenly, upon seeing something flash before her eyes, Darya cried out, "Wait! Wait!"

It was extremely important for her to re-experience what was inside this train car, as it held the memory of one of the most beautiful days in Darya's entire life: the first day of school.

Darya ran to catch up with the train car.

She remembered how happy she was to go to school, and how she had been in such a hurry to learn how to read and write back then.

Darya thought of all the treasured and unexpected things awaiting her in that train car.

Even as a child, Darya had known that school and learning could help her get closer to her dream of riding on the clouds and getting to the city of wishes in the sky. As she looked into the train car, Darya saw her childhood self studying hard, but she was interrupted again by the noise from another train car fast approaching.

She heard someone call out her name. Darya peered warily into the window of the next train car and, to her amazement, found a memory of herself in there as a schoolgirl jumping happily in the air.

Her cries of happiness could be heard from miles away -- there was just no way she could contain herself. This was an unforgettable moment:

Darya had won an award for being top of her class, and had been given an official certificate which read "Top Student of the Class."

After the ceremony, Darya watched her younger self run home to show her mother the certificate.

Darya was so full of emotion and could hardly believe that she had won. What she really needed was to hear her mom read the certificate out loud; in her mind, that was the only thing that would make it feel real.

As she watched herself running to find her mom, Darya had a strange feeling that something unexpected was about to happen, but she couldn't remember what it could be.

As soon as she looked into the train car where her mother sat working, however, all the memories rushed back to her. Darya ran into her mother's arms gleefully, proudly holding up the certificate she had just won.

Then she folded her arms and held her head high, looking as though she had just scaled a high mountain.

Darya beamed, "Look what I just won at school! Read it!"

Her mom smiled sweetly, silently staring at the certificate.

Darya could see a quizzical look on her mother's face. In that moment, it was so hard for Darya to be patient.

She asked again: "Mom, see what's written there? Read it out loud!"

Her mother stayed silent for another moment, then said softly, "I can't read this."

Darya couldn't believe what she was hearing and kept staring at her mother, waiting for a different response. She felt confused.

Then her mother spoke again in a low voice, "I don't know how to read or write."

Darya would never forget that day. It had been so hard for her to believe what she heard.

Her whole life, Darya had imagined that her mother was good at everything; how could she not know how to read or write?

At that moment, Darya felt the presence of all the characters from her mother's stories in that very train car.

They had all crowded in and were speaking in loud voices. Darya couldn't tell anymore which voices were real and which were imaginary.

She watched as the younger Darya asked her mother gently, "You never went to school? Didn't you want to learn?" Her mother forced a smile. "There were no schools where I grew up," she replied softly. "I was born in a really small village where nobody could read or write," she continued.

Darya played back what her mom was saying, repeating the sentences to herself to make sure she hadn't misheard anything. Seeing the effect this news was having on Darya, her mom tried to save the moment.

"I still achieved my childhood dream, though! All I ever wanted was to get out of that small village and live somewhere with schools for children to learn in."

Darya, still shocked and confused, asked, "Then why didn't you just come here sooner so that you could also go to school?"

Her mom responded, "Well, I asked my father many times, but he would always say that the village was our motherland. We had roots in that land.

He would say, 'If we leave, we can't take our home, our family, or our friends with us. Humans, like trees, should stay where their roots are.

If you are separated from your roots, you may easily fall.

A flower is always happiest when it's attached to its stem and roots. Even in the most beautiful, expensive vase, a flower cut from its roots will not survive.'"

"Then how did you ever get here?"

"This was my childhood dream, and it grew with me over the years. It wasn't until my dream grew big enough that it was finally able to carry me with it and bring me here, to the town and life I had always imagined."

Darya asked, "Do dreams live in our hearts or our minds?"

Darya's mom pondered the question for a moment, and then said, "Dreams are born in our minds. But in order for dreams to become a reality, they must travel from our minds to our hearts. Not all dreams can survive this journey.

Some turn back mid-way. Others just disappear or never start the journey at all; these dreams are easily forgotten. However, the dreams that finally reach our hearts are the best ones, the ones we love the most and the ones we will never forget."

Darya asked, "What happens to the dreams that finally make it to our hearts? "Her mother replied, "Those dreams are placed carefully into boxes within our hearts.

We lock those boxes with love and care, and make sure to keep them safe so that we can reopen them easily at the right time. The dreams that are locked into boxes without love, the ones that are tinged instead with doubt or disappointment, can never be unlocked and therefore never come true."

Darya asked, "What are the dreams in those boxes waiting for?" Her mother replied, "The dreams wait for us to imagine them coming true. If we try our hardest to see our dreams come true, then our dreams gain power, break through their locks, and rise straight towards the clouds in the skies. That is when they're finally able to pull us up with them so we can ride on the clouds alongside our dreams."

The train moved slowly now, as if it were carrying a heavy load. The next train car was filled with the feelings of homesickness that Darya's mom felt.

Retelling her life story and the journey of her dreams evoked memories of Darya's mom's own childhood, of the great days she had had while growing up in her beautiful, small, green village where everyone and everything was familiar.

Throughout her adult life Darya's mom had constantly thought of the memories, friends, and family that she had left behind in that village when she moved to the city. Darya's mother told her that even the clouds, the flowers, and the trees in her childhood village knew her and looked to her as a familiar friend.

Darya remembered feeling worried and asking her mother, "Does this mean you're not happy here?"

Her mother replied, "I will always miss what I left behind in the village, but that doesn't mean that I am not truly happy here. What makes me happy is seeing that you can live in a place where everyone can go to school. It makes me feel like my own dream has come true." Then she paused for a moment and continued, **"Sometimes, it's possible to give your dream as a gift to someone you love."**

This made both of them smile. But deep in Darya's eyes, there was no genuine joy. Darya remembered gazing at the sunset later that day, but it was a different sunset than all the others she had known.

That night, Darya couldn't sleep. She kept thinking about her mom's dream, turning it over and over in her mind. By the time her mom had moved from the village to the city, she was past school-age, and had to work all day. How could she still claim to be content, even after giving away her biggest childhood dream to someone else? Was she truly happy in her decision? Twisting and turning, Darya thought about something else her mother had said -- "Lots of people may have the exact same dream as you.

While it's true that you can reach happiness by only focusing on achieving your own dreams, imagine the kind of happiness that comes from helping others achieve their dreams! That type of happiness is even more special."

Darya had always dreamed of riding on a cloud to the city of dreams in the sky, but she had never considered the possibility that she could share a piece of her dream with others so that they could also ride among the clouds with her. "That can't be easy!" she thought to herself. Lost in her thoughts, Darya finally fell asleep.

Another train car made its way toward the present-day Darya, carrying the events of a beautiful morning full of light. The whole train car glittered with the warmth of morning sunlight, and Darya was barely awake when she suddenly remembered what she had been dreaming about the whole night. She had dreamt that her own hopes and deepest dreams had taken form and become close friends with her mother's dreams. She remembered that those dreams had been talking amongst themselves, discussing a completely new dream the whole night.

The Darya in the train car jumped from her bed. She wracked her brain, wanting to make sure that she had not lost sight of her original dream. As she was searching her thoughts she found it lying there, but it had changed... Darya noticed that it had perhaps grown a little bigger. She now had a new idea.

Darya wanted to wrap up her original dream of riding a cloud in imaginary boxes and give the boxes as gifts, just like the gift her mother had given to her. The thought of the joy she could bring to others with those gifts made Darya smile again. Holding tight to this new wish, Darya left the train car and ran off to find ways to make other people's dreams come true.

After that, every other car on the train looked to be filled with wishing clouds. These wishing clouds were all dreams that were once living at the bottom of Darya's heart, but now they were rising up and finding their way to the sky.

As each cloud passed, Darya reached out her hand; they were so close that she could grab onto any one if she reached out far enough.

Any time Darya could, she grabbed a cloud and climbed aboard, holding tight so she wouldn't fall off. It made her so happy to look down.

She loved seeing the world from this height.

From her seat atop the clouds of her wishes, she would often notice some people struggling to reach for their own clouds.

This was when Darya would float over and help them reach their dreams so that they too could ride on their clouds. This filled her with immense joy.

Her mom had been right; this kind of happiness was different from any other.

Each time she helped someone, it made her feel lighter,
which then lifted her higher and higher into the sky. At one point, one of the wishing clouds in the sky asked Darya, "How on earth did you make it so high up?"Darya answered, "Whenever I help others reach their dreams, their happiness makes me lighter. The lighter I feel, the higher up I go!" The old cloud started laughing, "But if their happiness makes you lighter and allows you to rise higher into the sky, then aren't they the ones helping you?" Darya was slightly taken aback and didn't know how to answer the cloud's question.

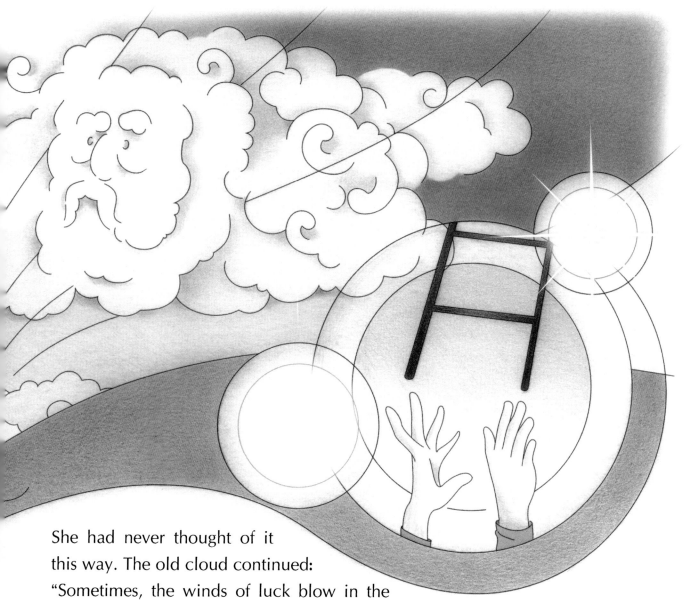

She had never thought of it
this way. The old cloud continued:
"Sometimes, the winds of luck blow in the
sky. They can push your cloud of wishes high above those of others. If you have the
chance to experience those winds, then you are given the opportunity to help others
reach their dreams. The more you help, the lighter you feel, and the higher up you
go. So, if you really think about it, by helping them you are really just helping
yourself." Darya felt confused.

She didn't know what to say to the old cloud in response. She needed to be alone, to
think about what she had just heard. The more Darya thought, the more she realized
that what the old cloud had said was true -- the chance to help others was a valuable
gift from the winds of luck that roamed the sky of wishes. Darya knew that it was a
priceless gift, and she felt blessed and thrilled to have been granted it.

As Darya grew up, her wishes grew with her and took her further and further into the sky. However, the higher she flew, the further away she got from those familiar childhood train cars. She missed sitting in the train cars and soaking in all those good memories. But she knew that the clouds only moved forward, never backwards. Darya kept rising higher and higher and eventually, she could see the other side of the world from the top of the clouds. A big city sprawled before her, hidden between large mountains. Darya remembered hearing about this city on the other side of the world, and knew that it was filled with new and dazzling things.

Now, it was finally right in front of her eyes. As she looked over the city, she recognized how distinctive and bright the colors were compared to her own modest little town. There were so many glittering lights that the whole city shone brightly before her. Was this the same magical city her mom used to tell stories about? If so, that would mean that the people who lived here could do amazing things, including pulling clouds of dreams down from the sky and sharing those wishes among the people living there. Darya would have loved to be one of these people, living here and helping to share wishes.

Darya looked around at the magnificent clouds above the dazzling city, thinking that perhaps they could help her achieve this goal so that she could do even more to help others. As much as she wanted to get to those clouds and ask them her questions, she also didn't want to distance herself too much from her train; it was as if the train cars carrying her memories were holding her back from going out any further.

She finally decided to try and speak to the clouds above the city from where she was sitting. She shouted, "Hey there! Do you see that faraway city? Can you tell me what the people living there do? How do they live? Are they happy?"

One of the biggest clouds in the sky answered back: "Hmm... people here seem to be busy working all the time. Some of them don't even have a moment to look up into the sky or search for their own clouds of wishes. Each day looks just like the last, but they all dream of a life where they can work less and have a chance to enjoy what they've earned."

Darya was surprised. "You mean they don't look for their clouds of wishes? They don't try to pursue their dreams?"

The big cloud continued, "They all have the option to look for their dreams, but there are so few of them who actually try to reach the biggest clouds. Those who do reach the clouds bring them back to earth, cut them up into smaller wishes, and share them among those who can't or don't try to reach their own clouds of dreams.

They give them to the ones who are lost in their repetitive working days, unable to reach their own dreams for so long that they have simply forgotten about them. Still, it is extraordinary to see how happy those hardworking people are when they receive those small shares of a wishing cloud!"

Darya was thrilled. "It's amazing that there are people in the big city who can share wishing clouds with others! I would really love to do the same one day."

The big cloud became silent. He did not want to tell Darya that these small pieces of wishing clouds were not given for free. The truth was, the hardworking people of the shimmering city were paying for these small pieces of the wishing clouds with their days and nights of toil.

Darya was full of excitement. "I'd like to go there! I want to live there! But it's so far from all the people I know and it will be difficult to leave everyone and everything behind. Can I bring my family, belongings, and accomplishments with me?"

Another cloud began laughing. "You can take whatever belongings you like as long as they can fit in one suitcase.

But you can't bring anyone with you. You'll just need to carry everyone's memories with you in your heart. However, keep in mind that if the burden of your memories becomes too heavy, you'll be stuck within the new city, unable to lift up into the sky full of big dreams.

Darya couldn't believe what she was hearing, and she became slightly irritated. "I might be able to fit all my belongings into one suitcase, but there's no way I can leave even a single memory behind. My memories are a large part of what has led me here."

The cloud replied gently, "Some of those memories will only make you happy in your old town. If you bring them with you to the big city, they will only serve as a burden of faraway sorrow. Do not worry yourself with these memories. Leave them behind in your old town. You may not believe this, but there are a great number of cities all around the world filled with people's past memories. The people who own those memories love them as well, but they live far away from them! The cities know exactly how to take care of their people's memories. Lighten your burden so that you can rise up higher."

35

Again, Darya felt confused. She knew that it wouldn't have been possible to reach the cloud of her childhood wishes if her mom had not left her own small village.

On the other hand, Darya also thought about all the time she had spent in her own town, and how hard she had worked to reach her dreams while there.

It was going to be really hard to leave everything behind, move to a faraway city, and start from scratch.It was a strange moment. Darya felt like she had been climbing a mountain for years, trying to reach the peak, and now, after finally standing on the peak, she finds out that she would have to climb yet another mountain.

From all the way up there, it seemed too hard for her to go back down and start climbing another mountain again. Darya thought hard about what the big city clouds told her, but she couldn't accept it. She wanted to consult with the clouds of her own city and ask them what they thought. She turned to go back, but the sky above her city was extremely polluted.

There was a gray layer of smoke everywhere. Not only were the clouds missing from the sky, but it was almost impossible to see the sun. Darya was disappointed that she couldn't speak to the wishing clouds in the sky of her own town and consult with them. She looked back across the sky, where the white clouds of the dazzling city were waiting for her. Finally, she made up her mind, and left.

This time, as she rode on a cloud away from her home city, Darya smiled, full of hope, even though her eyes were filled with tears at the thought of missing her hometown and the many memories she had had there. She whispered to herself, "I am just going to have to look forward from now on – I can't look back again." Even with this new resolve, she felt as if her eyes were drawn to what she was leaving behind. The more she looked forward, the more she saw her past. It was a bittersweet feeling. She tried imagining different shapes in the passing clouds to distract herself, but it was not helping.

Her vision blurred with tears when the clouds in the sky took on the shape of her home, her dog, her favorite flowers in the backyard, or her little goldfish that she had had a hard time saying goodbye to.

Darya was immersed in her thoughts when suddenly a white cloud in the shape of a giant pair of scissors appeared from the other side of the sky, approaching her.

"I may be able to help you. I think you need some scissors, to cut the rope that's connecting you to the train of your past memories," it said. "You won't be able to rise any higher in the sky while you are attached to that train. Cut the rope and it'll help you become lighter. Then, you will continue to rise up." Darya did not like what she was hearing at all. She did not want to cut ties with the memories of her childhood city. She just looked at the scissor-shaped cloud with sad eyes and remained silent.

****

Back in the delivery room, Darya's baby girl cried out just then, and Darya descended quickly from her imaginary wishing cloud. In the blink of an eye, the clouds disappeared and the train of memories was nowhere to be found. Darya was happy, nonetheless; during her imaginary venture in the clouds, she had been able to find the smile that she had lost in childhood among the train cars and bring it with her back into reality. Darya shone as beautifully as the sun with her big, warm smile, and a light in her eyes that only a new mother could have. With an excited feeling she could not name, Darya nursed her baby. It was a chance to gaze down at her baby girl's face, something she had wanted to do for so long now. Darya still couldn't believe how familiar her baby's face looked to her.

Since the day Darya had left behind her old town and arrived

in the dazzling big city on the other side

of the world, she had not seen a face as familiar

as her baby girl's.

Darya thought back to her first few days in the new city.

She had felt like a tree with no roots, constantly having to be careful so as not to fall.

She tried hard to steady herself by planting new, small roots, trying with all her might to ensure that she remained upright. She wanted so badly to hold her head high in the sky again and to be able to talk to the clouds of her dreams. One day, she tried to talk to a small piece of cloud sitting alone somewhere in the corner of the sky. Strangely, the cloud did not hear what she had to say -- or maybe it just did not understand what she was saying.

Darya's heart sank. She thought to herself, "What if the clouds in the sky of this city speak another language, just like the people here?"

The language in this new city was completely different from Darya's mother tongue. Since the moment Darya had arrived here, she had wished that she had some extra time to attend school and really learn the new language, but the long, repetitive work days had not given her that chance. Still, Darya knew that this couldn't be the case with the clouds. She knew that in the sky, everyone spoke with their heart.

They could convey the message of a thousand words, even in silence.

Since Darya's baby girl had been born, the sun somehow shone warmer

and brighter. Darya was truly happy that now she had someone at home to speak in her own childhood language with. She talked constantly to her baby, and although her daughter was too small to respond just yet, Darya was sure that she could understand what she said.

Darya worked hard every day and rarely had enough time to pay a visit back to the clouds of her dreams and imagination. Yet every night, she found time to sing songs to her baby girl and tell her stories.

Sometimes these stories were the same as those that her own mother used to tell her, or else stories about her friends in her old town. Mostly, however, Darya told her daughter about her own mother's kindness, a mother to whom she said goodbye to many years ago.

41

Days passed by and Darya's little girl grew up quickly. She loved drawing and painting. She especially loved to draw all of her mother's stories of an imaginary town. In all her drawings, she always first drew a big, warm, shiny sun surrounded by beautiful, white, fluffy clouds. She would name each of the clouds according to its shape: the elephant cloud, the airplane cloud, the angel cloud, and so on. The clouds in the little girl's drawings were always searching for new friends on earth. Just like in her mother's stories, these clouds liked to help people on earth reach their dreams.

In all her drawings, everything and everybody knew each other well. The flowers, the trees, and the clouds were like close friends.

The strangest thing about her drawings, however, was that each one featured a round, feathery dandelion who traveled all around the drawings and delivered good news. Anywhere the dandelion stopped the people would get happy and excited because they knew the dandelion always brought good news with her.

It was as if the dandelion was aware of everyone's wishes and what would make each person happy, and delivered them exactly that. One day, while the little girl was busy drawing, one of the clouds in her drawing asked her, "What is your biggest wish?" She replied quickly, without needing any time to think: "I would love to be like the dandelion and give everyone good news wherever I go."

The cloud told the little girl, "What a lovely wish! I love when humans have such beautiful dreams and aspirations. I even remember your mother's childhood dreams, and how hard she used to try to reach them. Nothing could ever stop her."

The little girl swelled with happiness after hearing this, and was even more proud of her mom than before. She could guess from what she had heard of her mom's life stories that her mother was not afraid of any obstacles, and that she had happily reached her cloud of wishes.

Days passed. The little girl would go to the imaginary town contained within her drawings every day, adding some new colors or drawing new events.

One day, the dandelion in the drawing approached the little girl from the corner of a colorful page. She smiled beautifully and told her that she had some good news for her. "It's almost time for one of the best days of your life," the dandelion said, "The first day of school!"

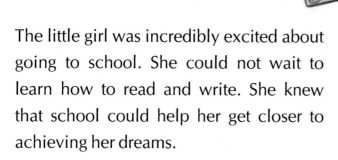

The little girl was incredibly excited about going to school. She could not wait to learn how to read and write. She knew that school could help her get closer to achieving her dreams.

When school began, the little girl studied hard, but also continued drawing and painting as usual.

One day, she drew a portrait of her mom; in the drawing, her mom was jumping high in the air because she had received exciting news. The little girl also wanted to add herself in the drawing, giving her mom the good news.

But no matter how hard she tried to think about it, she could not think of news that would make her mom that happy.

So, she drew a dandelion there instead, and waited until she could decide what news to surprise her mom with.

As it turned out, she would not have to wait long.

On a beautiful spring day with the smell of cherry blossoms in the air, some good news awaited the little girl in an envelope on her desk in class. In it was an award for the best drawing in the school drawing competition. The little girl was overjoyed at having won the award, and her thoughts shifted back to the drawing she did of her mom jumping in the air with happiness. Now, she finally had a good reason to add herself to that drawing.

She counted down the seconds until she could give her mom the news. It was so hard to be patient. She kept trying to imagine what her mom's reaction would be after seeing the award.

As soon as school ended, she ran all the way back home. She found her mom sitting there and jumped happily into her arms, proudly showing Darya the certificate that her teacher had given her.

Then she folded her arms and held her head high, looking as though she had just scaled a high mountain.

The little girl beamed, "Look what I just won at school! Read it!" Darya smiled sweetly, silently staring at the certificate.

The little girl could see a quizzical look on her mother's face.

She could not wait a second longer; she wanted so badly to see Darya's reaction so that she could finish her drawing of her jumping for joy into the air.

She asked again, "Mom, see what's written there? Read it out loud!"

Darya stayed silent for another moment, then said softly, "I can't read this."

The little girl couldn't believe what she was hearing and kept staring at her mother, waiting for a different response.

Darya repeated in a lower voice, "I don't know how to read or write in this language."

Acknowledgment

It's crazy that it took a pandemic for me to finally find enough time to achieve one of my life long goals -- writing a book.

This pandemic stopped all travel around the world, but gave me the time to commit my feelings to paper in the hopes of reaching immigrants across the globe.

So, I want to first thank all of the immigrants who have shared their stories with me.

I also want to thank my husband and my daughter, who supported and encouraged me throughout this process,

Zari Baniasadi, my high school friend, who helped me every step of the way on the road to publishing my first book,

Farshid M. Amani, the most cooperative illustrator who worked tirelessly to bring the feelings in this story to life,

Akie Hirsa and Hamid Kamali for dedicating a portion of their precious time to this project,

and Panteha Healey and Famy Chavosh for editing the book with love and patience.

Maryam Ebrahimi was born in Iran and immigrated to America over 20 years ago. She studied Industrial Design as an undergrad and received a master's degree in Art Research. Prior to coming to the US, Maryam taught at an art university in Iran and also used to write her own works as well as edit the works of others in her native language, Farsi.

Maryam currently lives in California and works as a business consultant at a major financial institution. In her free time, she enjoys both interior and landscape design.

This book is Maryam's first experience expressing her thoughts in a language that is not her native tongue. It is meant to showcase a common experience known to immigrants across the globe.

To learn more about Maryam and her work, visit www.ebrahimimaryam.com.

Farshid M. Amani studied Industrial Design as an undergraduate and master's student in Iran. Before becoming an illustrator, he worked in graphic design and exhibition design for a multitude of companies. For this story, he began by focusing on composition and structure, ensuring that the layout of the images truly aligned with the emotions of the story before fine-tuning the drawings themselves.

The simplicity of his monochrome images allows for the idea behind each image to be brought to the fore. When Farshid does chose to bring in color, it is chosen with deliberation and truly adds meaning to the image.

Although he has utilized a wide range of styles throughout his career, Farshid was able to work closely with the author to bring this story to life exactly as the author envisioned it. To see more of Farshid's work, visit www.mohsenamani.com.